Does this book belong to **you** 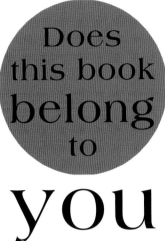?

Yup!

Then you can write your name **here:**

....

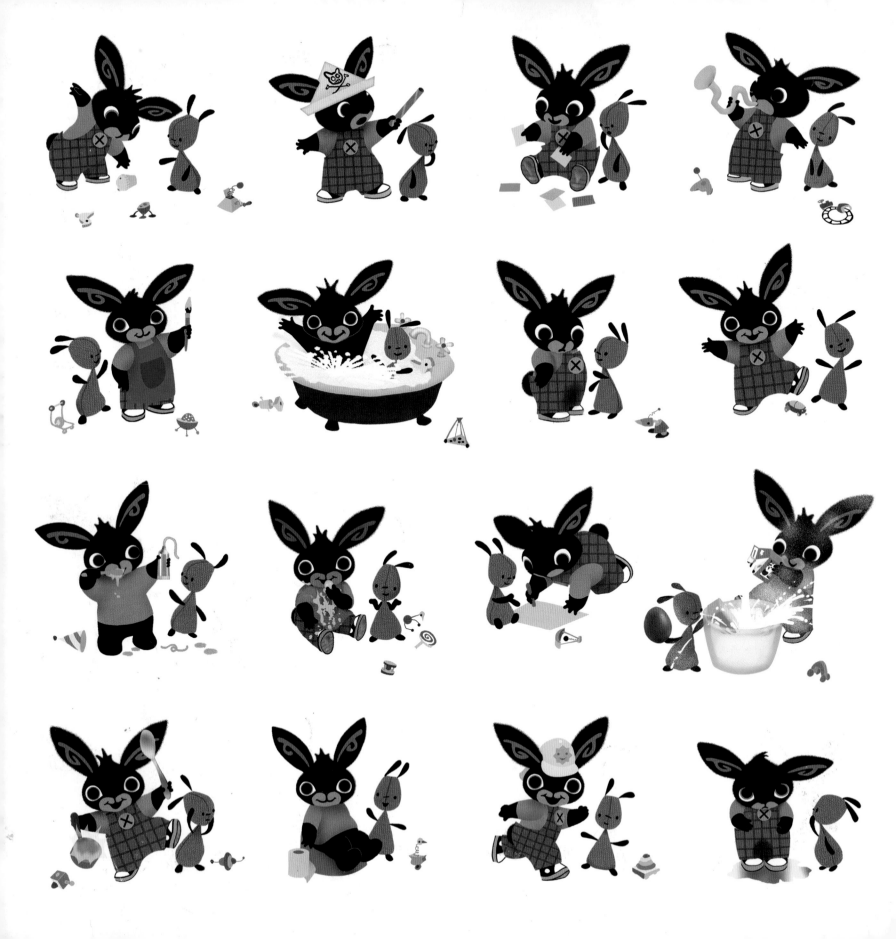

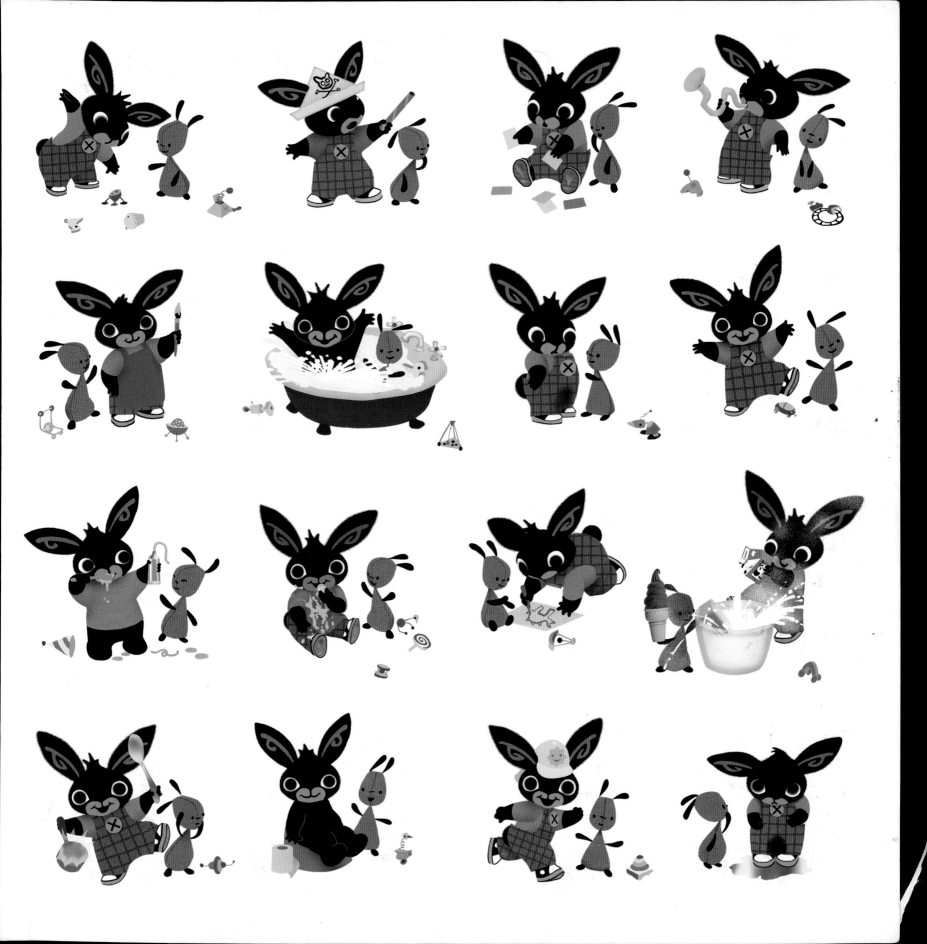

Ready to Read?

Yup!

Bing

Something for Mummy

by
Ted Dewan

HarperCollins *Children's Books*

**Round the corner,
Not far away,
It's another be nice
To Mummy day.**

How would you like to do something nice for Mummy?

YUP!

What would be
nice for Mummy?

Juice with a
bendy straw?

How about:

 juice with a bendy straw

and  happy jammy toast

and pretty flowers?

YUP!

OK, Let's go!

First, let's get **juice** and a cup...

and a **tray** to put them on.

NOW make
toast.

Bread
in the
toaster.

yum yum
yummy

Is it nice?

YUP!

Mummy will love that, Bing.

Stick in a
bendy
straw.

Oops.

It's spilly.

But some got into the cup.

...to pick **pretty flowers.**

Dandelions!

Is it nice?

YUP!

Mummy will love that, Bing.

uh-oh

What's that burny smell?

Oh no! We forgot about the toast.

It's all burny.

Don't worry, Bing.
It's no big thing.

Let's cover up
the burny bits...

...with jam!

It will be nice when you bring Mummy...

juice with a bendy straw

and happy jammy toast

and pretty flowers

because
you did it
with love...

and love

is a Bing Thing.

What would be nice for **your** mummy?

pretty flowers

roundy egg

puppet show

juice with a straw

snappy carrot

clothespeg doll

sweet kiss

shiny pebble

pasta necklace

fun banana

jammy toast

dancy music

lovely art

Bing again? Yup!

978-0-00-751477-9

978-0-00-751479-3

978-0-00-751540-0

978-0-00-751542-4

978-0-00-751544-8

978-0-00-751546-2

by
Ted Dewan

First published in paperback in Great Britain by HarperCollins Children's Books in 2017.   1 3 5 7 9 10 8 6 4 2   ISBN: 978-0-00-821201-8
HarperCollins Children's Books is a division of HarperCollins Publishers Ltd. Text and illustrations copyright © Ted Dewan 2017. The author/illustrator asserts the moral right to be identified as the author/illustrator of the work.